This book belongs to

....

....

The friends

Peter the Penguin
Pom the Panda

Benny the Cat   Teddy the Bear

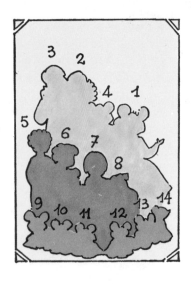

1. Mary Mouse
2. Mummy Doll
3. Daddy Doll
4. Whiskers Mouse
5. Pip
6. Melia
7. Roundy
8. Jumpy
9. Woffly
10. Scamper
11. Patter
12. Squeaker
13. Tiny
14. Frisky

Mary Mouse goes to sea

Enid Blyton

RAVETTE BOOKS

Printed and bound for Ravette Books Limited,
3 Glenside Estate, Star Road
Partridge Green, Horsham
West Sussex RH13 8RA
An Egmont Company
in Great Britain

ISBN: 1 85304 349 4

Contents

Chapter 1

Daddy Doll Wins a Prize

Who
is this
running
down a road
somewhere in France? Who has a
little grey head, a pointed nose, some
fine whiskers and two little round
ears? Yes, it is Mary Mouse. She is
wearing a black hat with a feather
and a red jacket over her black skirt.
What is she waving in her hand as
she runs back to the little Doll's

House? It is a letter.

"This letter is for Daddy Doll," she said. "The postman says it is very important." Mary ran into the house and gave the letter to Daddy Doll.

Daddy Doll took the letter and sat down on a chair. Mummy Doll and Melia sat beside him. Carefully he put his glasses on and opened the letter.

Pip and Roundy watched him with Jumpy the dog.

"Listen!" said Daddy Doll. "I've won a prize. I shall soon have a lot of money!" Everyone danced for joy. Melia danced with Jumpy, little Roundy danced with Mummy Doll. Pip  danced with Daddy Doll. Mary Mouse ran down to her little home in the cellar to tell her six children Frisky, Scamper and Squeaker who were boys and Woffly, Patter and Tiny, the girls. Then they all went into the garden to tell Mary's husband, Whiskers the gardener.

"What shall we buy?" they all cried.

"A pony!" said Melia.

"No! A monkey!" said Pip.

"No, no! A kitten!" said Roundy.

"It shall be a secret till I buy it — whatever it is!" said Daddy Doll, and he put on his hat. He went off down the road to collect the money. Whatever will he buy with it?

In the evening Daddy Doll came back.

"Come and see what I've bought," he said. So off they all went following Daddy Doll.

Daddy Doll took them down to the river. He led them onto a stone jetty and there — safely tied to a big iron post — was a big sailing ship.

"What a beautiful ship!" cried the children. "Can we go on it?"

"Yes. It's ours! I bought it with my prize money," said Daddy. "It's called Sea Foam."

"Ours! A ship of our very own!"

cried Pip. "I am so glad you bought it."

"Come on board," said Daddy Doll. "Look, here is the wheel to steer it with."

Pip took hold of the big wheel. The others went down below decks. Melia shouted in delight.

"Mummy, look! There are bunks to sleep in! May we sleep in them please?"

"I want to go to sea. I want to go

to sea!" cried Roundy, dancing about. "Can I be a sailor?"

"That is just what we are going to do," said Daddy Doll. "I used to be a sailor and I am going to take you all for a holiday. We shall go next week."

What an excitement there was! Mary Mouse took Melia, Pip and Roundy to the shops to buy sailor's clothes. All the mouse children went too. They bought warm jackets and waterproof trousers. They did look grand.

At last the time came for the holiday to begin. They all went on board the ship and set the sails. Daddy Doll took the wheel. The children stood on deck and waved goodbye to their friends.

Soon the little ship was gliding down the river towards the sea.

Chapter 2

Off to Sea

Soon the sailing ship left the river and sailed out into the wide ocean.

"Now we shall have some adventures," said Roundy. He climbed on to the rail to look for fish — the ship hit a big wave and Roundy nearly fell overboard. Luckily Mary Mouse grabbed him

just as he fell. She was very cross
with him.

Daddy Doll gave the wheel to
Whiskers Mouse. He called all the
children round him.

"I'm the captain of our ship," he
said. "You must obey my orders.
Each of you will have jobs to do.
Whiskers will help me to steer the
ship and look after the sails. Mummy
Doll and Melia, you must keep the
bunks tidy. Mary Mouse will look
after the cooking in the galley.
Mouse children, you must scrub the
decks. And Pip and Roundy, you
will carry messages and take cups of
tea to the captain."

Everyone got on with their jobs.
The ship sailed on. Poor Jumpy was
seasick. Everyone else was very
happy. And the sea was quite calm.

One day they came to a little
island. They let down the anchor

and went ashore. Pip saw some tall trees.

"Look! There are coconuts!" he shouted.

The children picked up some stones and threw them at the coconuts. Some fell down and one fell on Daddy Doll's head. He sat down looking very surprised. They drank the milk out of the coconut and ate the white nut inside. It was very good.

They sailed on. One day Whiskers Mouse came running to Daddy Doll.

"Captain, our fresh water is running out!" he cried.

So the ship had to stop at another island for fresh water. They all went ashore in the little dinghy with buckets. Mary Mouse found a stream and they filled their buckets with cool clear water.

"We had better come back and fill them again," said Daddy Doll, as

they carried the
buckets to the
ship.

But just as
they were
filling their
buckets a
second time,
Mary heard
a strange noise. She stood up and
looked around. There, behind a
bush, she saw an enormous tiger.

It was Jumpy who saved them. He ran at the tiger and barked so fiercely that the tiger ran away in fright. The Doll family and the mice picked up their buckets and hurried back to the ship. Jumpy had a special dinner that day. He deserved it!

Once Pip had an adventure of his own. He went for a swim in the sea. Suddenly Mummy Doll saw an enormous fish coming up behind Pip.

She shouted loudly:

"Swim for the ship, Pip! That fish may eat you!"

How frightened everyone was!

But Pip liked the big fish. He climbed onto its back and went for a ride. Then the fish dived and left Pip splashing on the surface.

"It is alright," said Daddy Doll. "That is a dolphin, not a fish. It was playing a game with Pip."

Another time the ship sailed into a beautiful cove. The sea was calm and blue.

"What are those fish doing, sitting on a rock?" asked Roundy.

"I do believe they are mermaids," said Daddy Doll.

"I wish I could play with them," said Melia.

Back at sea the wind blew the ship along fast. Oh dear, Squeaker Mouse has climbed onto the rail! The ship rolled and Squeaker fell overboard. *Splash*! Who will save him?

Pip picked up a life belt and threw

it to Squeaker. He pulled him back into the ship. Mary Mouse hugged Pip and put Squeaker to bed in his bunk. He was safer there.

The next day Daddy Doll said, "There is going to be a storm. We must go home."

Too late! The sky went black with angry clouds and a strong wind began to blow. Mary told the children to go to their bunks. But every time the ship rolled they fell out again. Daddy Doll and Whiskers hauled in the sails and tried to steer the ship. Where were they going?

All night the ship tossed in the storm.

"Where are we going?" asked Mummy Doll. Daddy Doll didn't know.

"I've lost my way," he said. "I don't know how to get home."

The next morning, the wind dropped and the ship sailed into

calm waters.

"Land ahoy!" shouted Whiskers.
"I can see a river."

Soon the
ship was
sailing
into the
river.
And there

was the little stone jetty!

Who is standing on the jetty
waving to them? It is Teddy the
Bear, Pom the Panda, Peter the
Penguin and Benny the Cat.

"Why, we're home!" said Mary
Mouse. "The wind blew us safely
back."

How nice it was to be on dry land
again!

"But we did enjoy our
adventures!" said Mary Mouse.

Chapter 3

Mary
and her Bicycle

Soon everyone settled down after their holiday. Mary Mouse was happy to be home. She scampered all over the house sweeping, dusting, cooking, washing up and mending clothes.

One day when she came back with the shopping, all the children crowded round her.

"Did you buy me an ice cream?" shouted Pip. "Oh good!"

"And did you get my sweets?" said Melia. "Thank you."

"And where's my ball?" asks Roundy. "Please, Mary Mouse!"

"I've brought the shopping too," said Mary Mouse, "and a newspaper for Daddy Doll."

Mary's children came running up. They got a lollipop each.

"Mary Mouse! Your basket is too heavy," said Daddy Doll, lifting it up. "What shall we do?"

The next day Daddy Doll called Mary Mouse.

"I have a surprise for you," he said. And there was a new bicycle leaning against the wall, waiting for her.

"Oh, how beautiful!" said Mary Mouse. "And there's a basket on the front for the shopping."

Mary Mouse had to learn how to ride the bicycle. First she got on, then she pushed the pedals with her feet and then she wobbled. Oh dear, Mary Mouse has fallen off!

"You've hurt your knee," said Melia. "I'll bandage it up."

"I don't like you to fall off your bicycle," wept Roundy.

"Well, you must help me to ride it then," said Mary. So Roundy did his best to help her.

Soon Mary could ride very well. Everyone was surprised to see her going so fast.

One day Mary Mouse went out shopping on her bicycle. She left it outside the grocer's shop. But when she came out, it had gone. What a dreadful shock!

Mary Mouse went to tell the policeman. He took out his notebook and wrote it all down. Then Mary went sadly home and told everyone what had happened.

Pip, Melia and Roundy were very sorry for Mary. Melia hugged her.

"We'll get it back for you," she said.

So they all went out to look for the thief. They looked at every bicycle outside the shops, but not one was Mary's.

"We'll save up and buy her another one," said Pip, getting down his money box.

They all put in their Saturday pennies. Then Pip went to Pom the Panda and began to work in his garden. He weeded and dug and watered, and Pom the Panda paid him.

Melia went to see Mrs Teddy Bear, and took her five babies for a walk in their pram. But when Melia lifted them out to look at the ducks in the pond, the smallest bear ran away, and Melia didn't see him go. So when she took the baby bears back home there were only four.

Luckily, Roundy had met the naughty little bear and he took his paw and walked him all the way home. So Melia got paid too. Roundy found some work too. He took his little tricycle and went to fetch Peter the Penguin's shopping every day. And except when he upset a basket of apples that went rolling away, he was a splendid errand boy, and Peter the Penguin paid him well.

Daddy Doll said he would help too. He put on his sailor's hat and took people for trips in a big rowing boat on the river. He got plenty of money.

Mummy Doll made a lovely blue

coat for Benny the Cat. It had twenty eight buttons down the front.

Mary's children helped too. Squeaker delivered the newspapers. Scamper cleaned Teddy the Bear's windows. Patter and Woffly darned socks for everyone. And Frisky and Tiny peeled potatoes for the school dinners.

"I must do something to help too," said Whiskers Mouse. So he got a job polishing the toy railway engine. He made it shine like a mirror.

"I can see my face in it," said Whiskers. What a lot of money he made!

By the end of the month, the money box was full. Daddy Doll counted it. There was just enough to buy a bicycle.

"Tomorrow we will go and buy your new bicycle, Mary!" he said.

But, oh dear! That night

somebody crept up to the Doll's House. He tried the back door, but it was locked. He tried the front door, but that was bolted as well as locked. He tried the downstairs windows, but they were safely fastened.

Then he got a ladder and set it against the house. He climbed up to an open window. He crept in. The children were fast asleep in bed. They did not stir. The burglar tiptoed downstairs and found the money box. He put it under his arm and opened the front door. Then he went out into the night.

The next day when Daddy Doll looked for the money, it had gone.

"It's been stolen!" said Mary Mouse. "The front door is open."

"Look! There's a ladder going up to my window," said Pip.

Roundy cried, "I want Mary Mouse to have her bicycle."

"Never mind, I might fall off again and hurt myself," said Mary.

Pip went out into the garden. First he found the footprints in the flowerbed. Then he found a big red button.

"Melia, Roundy — look!" he cried. "The burglar must have dropped this. If we can find someone who has lost a big red button from his coat, he will be the thief." So the children went off to look.

Roundy met the milkman. His coat had red buttons. But all the buttons were there.

Melia met Miss Pig. She was wearing a smart red dress. But it had no buttons at all, only a belt.

But Pip suddenly met Zephyr, the monkey. On his jacket were big red buttons. And one was missing.

"You have lost a red button, Zephyr," said Pip.

"Rude boy!" said Zephyr, and

pushed him hard. But Pip wasn't afraid, and followed him back to his house. Pip peeped through the window. There on the table was their money box!

Pip ran back to the Doll's House and told everyone. Daddy Doll went to fetch the policeman. Soon the policeman was banging on Zephyr's front door.

"Open the door!" he shouted. But Zephyr jumped out of the window at the back and got on a bicycle and rode away fast.

"That's my bicycle!" shouted Mary Mouse.

Zephyr turned round to see if they were following and fell off — bump! The policeman and Daddy caught him and marched him off to the police station. The children looked for the money box. At last Melia found it in a saucepan. All the money was there.

"Now we've got the money *and* your bicycle too!" cried Pip dancing round.

"I shall ride off on my bicycle and do a bit of shopping," said Mary

Mouse. So, with the money box under her arm, off she went on the bicycle.

And when she came back, she had a doll for Melia, a train for Pip, a ship for Roundy and a ball for each of the mouse children. There were presents for Daddy Doll and Mummy Doll too, and a big handkerchief for Whiskers.

Good old Mary Mouse!

Chapter 4

Pip's Birthday

One day Mary Mouse came down early in the morning. She went into the kitchen and shut the door, and began to make a cake. She took some eggs and some sugar and flour and some fruit. She mixed everything together. Then she opened the oven door and put the mixture in the oven.

What is she making? It is a birthday cake. When it came out of the oven, Mary made some icing and covered the cake all over. Then she found six candles and put them on the cake. One, two, three, four, five, six. Who is going to be six?

Mary wrote on the cake with icing sugar. It said *Happy Birthday Pip*. Yes, it's Pip's birthday.

Pip came dancing into the kitchen. "It's my birthday, Mary. Is that my cake?"

"You mustn't see it yet," said Mary Mouse. And she put it quickly into a cupboard. All the others came downstairs.

"Happy Birthday, Pip!" they shouted. Everyone had a parcel for Pip. There were such a lot.

Mummy Doll gave him a big bouncing ball. It flew right up to the ceiling.

"Thank you, Mummy," said Pip.

"I will play with it in the garden."

Daddy Doll gave him an alarm clock.

"That will wake you up in the morning," said Daddy Doll.

Whiskers gave him a kite.

"How lovely!" said Pip. "I shall fly it on the first windy day."

Then he opened a beautiful

clockwork train. It went all round the room. Melia and Roundy and the six mouse children had put all their money together to buy it for Pip.

Pip said thank you to everyone.

"What are you giving Pip, Mary Mouse?" asked Roundy, pulling at her apron.

"Aha!" said Mary. "I've got it outside. I'll fetch it. It's too big to wrap up.

Mary Mouse went out of the door and came back with . . . a smart new bicycle.

"Oh!" said Pip, "It's my very nicest present!" He gave Mary Mouse an enormous hug.

"I'll get on it," he said.

"No, no, don't ride indoors!" cried Mummy Doll.

But it was too late. Pip wobbled and fell over — *Crash*! And the grandfather clock fell over too, and the glass broke.

"If it wasn't your birthday, I would spank you," said Daddy Doll picking up the clock.

"I'll go and ride in the road," said Pip, and he wheeled his bicycle to the door.

"No, no!" cried Mary Mouse. "You must learn the rules of the road first, Pip!"

"Quite right," said Mummy Doll, and Pip had to take his bicycle to the shed.

Pip had a lovely birthday. When the postman came, he brought Pip ten cards and four more parcels. In the afternoon, Mary lit the six candles on Pip's birthday cake. It looked wonderful. Pip took a deep breath and blew them all out. I wonder what he wished!

The next day Pip wheeled his bicycle into the road. Mary Mouse came too with her own bicycle.

"I shall teach you how to ride

properly," she said. "Now when you want to turn right, put your hand

out like this — and when you want to turn left, put out your hand, just like this. Ring your bell to warn anyone coming round the corner. That's right, Pip. And never hang on to the back of a van, as that silly boy is doing — look!" Oh dear! The van stopped suddenly and the boy crashed into it.

"What bruises he will have!" cried Mary Mouse, as she ran to pick up the silly boy.

She did not see Pip riding on by himself.

"I'm quite alright," he thought. "Why! I can even ride without holding on to the handle bars!"

But he began to wobble, so he had to take hold of them again. Then down the hill he went at top speed. Brake! Pip, brake! But Pip didn't brake because he liked going fast. And then round the corner came a big teddy bear. Pip rang his bell madly. But he was going too fast to stop. He crashed into the teddy bear, and fell off his bicycle with a bump. The bear fell over too and knocked his face on the kerb.

He yelled.

"I've knocked one of my beautiful glass eyes out! You bad boy, bumping me like that!"

Pip got up to get his bicycle.

"I'm sorry," he said. But the teddy bear got hold of his bicycle first.

"You find my lost eye for me!" he said. "Then you can have your bicycle."

So Pip looked and looked. But he

couldn't find the teddy bear's eye anywhere.

"It must have gone down this drain," said Pip.

"Oh! Is that so?" said the bear. "Well, I shall keep your bicycle then. Goodbye!" He rode off on it.

"Learn the rules of the road before you ride a bicycle again," he shouted.

Poor Pip had to walk all the way home. He was very unhappy.

Chapter 5

Mary Mouse has a Good Idea

When Pip arrived home he told Mummy and Daddy Doll what had happened. He was very ashamed. Mary Mouse was angry.

"It serves him right, Daddy Doll," she said. "He rode away from me before he had learned the rules of the road."

Pip cried and cried — a whole puddle of tears.

"I did so love my bicycle!" he wept.

"I'll buy it back from the bear. Where is my money box?"

But there wasn't enough money in it, though Melia, Pip and Roundy counted it again and again.

"We'll earn some money for you, Pip," said Melia kindly. "And you can earn some too." They set to work at once.

Pip took his little cart to Pom the Panda's house and did all Pom's shopping. Pom gave him five pennies.

Melia went mushrooming in the fields each morning very early. She carried a basket, and when it was full

she took it to the greengrocer's. He
gave her quite a lot of money too.

"It's all for you Pip," she said.

Little Roundy took his
wheelbarrow and went off to the
woods all by himself. He picked up
sticks until his barrow was full. Then
he took the sticks home and made
twelve little bundles. Roundy could
count to twelve. One, two, three,
four, five, six, seven, eight, nine, ten,

eleven, twelve. Roundy sold the bundles of sticks to Mummy Doll. She gave him a penny for each bundle.

At last the money box was quite full. Pip tipped it out on to the table.

"Yes," said Mummy Doll. "That will be enough to buy your bicycle back from the teddy bear."

Pip put the money in a bag and carried it to the teddy bear's house.

It was quite heavy.

Rat-a-tat-tat! Pip knocked on the bear's door. A big voice answered.

"Come in — and don't forget to wipe your feet!"

Pip opened the door. There was the teddy bear sitting in a big armchair, looking very fierce, even though he only had one eye to look fierce with. Pip put his bag of money on the table.

"I've come to buy my bicycle back," he said, emptying out the money, "and to say I'm very, very sorry."

"Take the money away," said the bear standing up crossly. "I don't want money. I want my eye back!"

He looked so cross that poor Pip gathered up the money and ran out of the door. He went home crying, and told Mummy Doll how fierce the teddy bear was and what he had said.

When Mary Mouse heard she was very sorry. That night when she tucked Pip up in bed, she said:

"If only you had been sensible and waited to learn the rules of the road!"

Then she went down to her little home in the cellar and talked to Whiskers.

"I once knew a bear who had two

boot button eyes. He looked fine!"
said Whiskers, as he cleaned the
shoes.

"Oh, what a good idea!" said
Mary Mouse. "Tomorrow I will go
to the shop and buy two big, black
boot buttons."

That evening she baked a
chocolate cake.

The next morning Mary Mouse
put on her hat and went into the
town. She bought two big, black boot
buttons and put them in a bag. Then
she returned home and got a needle
and a reel of cotton and the cake,
and put them in a bag too. She went
to the teddy bear's house and
knocked loudly.

"Come in and wipe your feet!"

Mary Mouse opened the door.

"Why, it's little Mary Mouse who
lives in the Doll's House and makes
lovely cakes!" said the bear.

"I've brought you one!" said

Mary. And she put the beautiful chocolate cake on the table. "And

I've brought you the latest fashion in eyes — lovely, black boot buttons. Look!"

Mary cut a big piece of cake for the teddy bear. And while he ate it, she quickly sewed and sewed. When she had finished, the teddy bear had

two fine, boot button eyes. He was so pleased. "Thank you, Mary," he said. "Here is the bicycle. I am sorry I was so cross about it."

Mary Mouse got on Pip's little bicycle and rode back home to the Doll's House. When she got to the front gate she rang the bell. Ting-a-ling-a-ling! Out ran Pip smiling all over his face.

"Oh! My lovely bicycle! You are clever, Mary Mouse!"

Then the children took the bag of money they had collected for the teddy bear and gave it to Mary

Mouse.

"It's for you!" they said. "What will you buy with it, Mary?"

"I shall buy a new hat," said Mary. And she went to the shop and bought a beautiful new hat covered with little flowers and birds.

"You deserve it, Mary!" said Pip, and he hugged her very hard.

Chapter 6

Noah's Ark

One morning Mary Mouse went to see Mummy Doll. She was very excited.

"There is a funny looking building on the grass near our house," she said.

Mummy Doll looked out of the window.

"Dear me!" she said. "It's a Noah's Ark! Let's go and look at it.

Isn't it grand! Look at all the
windows!"

Mummy Doll and Mary Mouse
went out. Soon they met a strange
man with a long white beard.

"Good morning," he said. "I am
your new neighbour. My name is Mr
Noah."

Mrs Noah came up too.

"Do come in," she said.

Mary Mouse went back to fetch
the children. Melia, Pip and Roundy
and the six little mice went into the
Noah's Ark with Mary and Mummy

Doll. What a noise there was inside!

"That is the animals," said Mrs Noah. "Come and see them all. Here are Mr and Mrs Lion. Do shake hands with the children!"

But Roundy was afraid. He ran away at top speed — and bumped into Mr and Mrs Kangeroo.

"Poor little boy. Are you frightened?" said Mrs Kangeroo, and she picked him up and put him

in the pocket she used for her babies.
He was surprised.

Then Melia met Mr and Mrs
Jumbo, the two elephants. Mr Jumbo
held out his trunk to shake hands —

and lifted Melia right up on to his
head with his trunk.

"Me too! Me too!" shouted
Roundy, jumping out of Mrs
Kangeroo's pocket, and Mrs Jumbo
lifted him up on *her* head.

"There isn't a Jumbo for me," said
Pip. "I'll ride on Mr Snake."

But it wasn't easy, as Mr Snake's
body curved in and out as he went
and Pip slid off his tail with a bump.

The six little mice were playing
hide-and-seek among the animals,

when a monkey came along ringing a bell.

"Time for our walk!" he cried.

The animals all lined up in twos and began to walk out of the Ark. There were two lions, two bears, two foxes, two giraffes, two ostriches, two camels, two elephants, two tortoises — more animals than the children could count. At the end of the line walked Pip and Melia, pretending that they were animals too.

By the end of the day, Mr and Mrs Noah were firm friends of Mary Mouse and Mummy Doll. They came to tea at the Doll's House and Mary Mouse made some marvellous cakes.

The two cats came to have tea with Melia. When Mary Mouse brought in some cakes, they chased her. Melia was angry.

"Go straight home, you naughty

cats!'' she said. They went back to
the Ark very ashamed of themselves.

The two frogs came to play with
Pip. They played leap-frog all
afternoon. And the two ducks came
to see Roundy. But when Mary
Mouse went to look for them, they
had disappeared. Roundy had taken

them upstairs for a swim in the bath..

Everyone was very happy with
their friends from the Noah's Ark.
But one day Roundy went by himself
to visit the ducks. He left the door
of the Ark open behind him. And out
poured all the animals, not even two
by two. They knocked Roundy over
and he sat in the Ark and howled.

Mr Noah came hurrying up.

"Good gracious me!" he said, "Where are all my animals?"

He ran to the Doll's House for help. Mary Mouse got out her bicycle and rode off to look for the animals, shouting as she went.

"Mr Lion! Mrs Bear! Mr Tiger! Mrs Giraffe! Mr Wolf! Where are you?" But no one replied.

At last she came to a great big tent that belonged to Mr Keen's Grand Circus. There was a terrible noise! And there, in a field behind the tent were all the Noah's Ark animals. They were talking happily to Mr Keen's circus animals. Mary rode back on her bicycle to tell Mr Noah.

"You must come quickly," she said, "or your animals will join the circus!"

Mr Noah came as quickly as he could. My goodness, he was cross!

The animals were frightened and they wouldn't go two by two. They ran here and there.

"I will deal with them," said Mr Keen. He took his big circus whip. *Crack*! What a noise the whip made!

"Form into twos!" shouted Mr Keen.

Straight away all the animals formed into pairs, one behind the other, as good as gold. First the lions, then the sheep, then the camels and the tortoises. But Mr Noah was very surprised to see that there were five elephants and seven horses and eight bears.

"Go back home!" he said to the circus animals. "Only the Noah's Ark animals may go into the Ark."

So the circus animals had to leave their new friends and go back to the circus.

Chapter 7

Mr Noah
is Unhappy

One day when Mary Mouse was
out shopping, she passed by the
Noah's Ark. And, dear me! There
was Mrs Noah, crying bitterly!
Mary Mouse stopped at once.

"What is the matter, Mrs Noah?"
she asked.

"Oh dear!" Mrs Noah sobbed.
"We've got to leave the Ark! You
see it needs repairing and repainting
and we haven't enough money."

Mr Noah was sad too.

"We'll have to send all the animals
to a zoo," he said, "and find a little
house for ourselves."

The animals heard what he said
and wept great tears. The giraffes
sobbed, the lions howled, the
elephants groaned. What a noise!

Mary was very upset. Poor Mr
and Mrs Noah! She hurried home to
the Doll's House.

The three children ran to meet
her.

"What's the matter?" asked Pip
and Melia.

Mary Mouse went to find Daddy
and Mummy Doll.

She told them about the Noah's
Ark and all the money that was
needed.

"It will certainly be a lot of money," said Daddy Doll.

"We must all try to think of an idea to help," said Mummy Doll.

That night they all thought hard about Mr Noah's problem.

In the morning Mary Mouse had an idea.

"Why don't we give a grand concert!" she said.

"We could give the money to Mr

Noah to mend the Ark," said Mummy.

"What a marvellous idea, Mary!" Everyone agreed. So a meeting was held at the Doll's House. Pom the Panda came. So did Benny the Cat and Teddy the Bear. They all gave their advice.

"I shall be a clown and walk on my hands," said Teddy the Bear.

"Benny and I will do a dance with Peter," said Pom the Panda, dancing round to show them.

"I'll sing nursery rhymes," said Roundy proudly. "I know two. Listen!"

"And I'll dance my fairy dance!" said Melia, standing on her tip toes.

"I'll conduct a band to play the music," said Pip, beating his drum.

"I'll teach Mary Mouse's children how to play the music."

Frisky, Scamper, Squeaker and Woffly, Patter and Tiny squeaked

with excitement. They couldn't wait
to begin.

"I'll help Mary Mouse to make all
the clothes," said Mummy Doll.

She went to get her work basket.

"I'll look after the stage and the
curtain and the lights," said Daddy
Doll. "And Whiskers Mouse can
help me."

Mary Mouse went to tell Mrs
Noah. Oh dear! She was packing her
cases already! The animals were
bringing her everything to pack.
They came up two by two. The two
lions were carrying a big carpet on
their backs. The ostriches brought
pots of flowers and the camels had
little bags.

"Now you just unpack again!"
said Mary Mouse, and she told Mrs
Noah all about the concert. The
animals dropped what they were
carrying and jumped for joy. The
snakes danced on their little boxes.

Mrs Noah was so happy that she sat down and cried for joy.

"You are so kind," she said, and began to unpack all the cases again.

What an excitement! Soon everyone was busy preparing for the concert. Pip beat his drum. Scamper and Squeaker practised their trumpets. Patter and Tiny played the

violin and Woffly played the piano.
Frisky had a little drum like Pip.
They made a very good band.

Melia practised her fairy dance
and spun round on her toes like a
top. Roundy sang his nursery rhymes
to Mummy Doll and Mary Mouse,
while they sewed all the dresses.

The day of the concert drew near.

"We'd better put up some big posters," said Daddy Doll.

Mummy Doll and Mary Mouse had finished all the dresses.

"We had better make some tickets," said Mummy Doll.

"I'll help you."

They made three lots of tickets. Some cost two pennies, some four pennies — and for the best seats, six pennies.

Mummy Doll gave the tickets to the children to sell. Off they went to the town with bags to put the money in.

Melia sold tickets to the butcher and the baker. They bought four each. Pip sold tickets to the school teacher. He bought six tickets because he had so many friends. Roundy sold two tickets to his friend, the sweep.

"I'm going to be a sweep one day," he said.

In the evening all the mouse children came back home with their money. Daddy counted it on to the table. There was such a lot!

"People who haven't got tickets can pay at the door, said Mummy Doll.

Daddy Doll and Whiskers Mouse made a big board.

At last the great day came.
Everyone knew their parts. All the
dresses were ready, and so was the
stage. The people began to come in
with their tickets. Some bought them
from Daddy Doll at the ticket office.
There was great excitement behind
the stage. Everyone got dressed for
their part. Melia couldn't find her
fairy wings. Oh dear! Roundy was
trying them on! Then he took

Frisky's drum. Behave yourself, Roundy!

"I'll send you home, Roundy, and you shan't say your nursery rhymes!" said Mary Mouse.

After that Roundy sat quietly, waiting for his turn.

The band began to play. Pip was conducting. The little mice were playing beautifully. Roundy recited Little Jack Horner very well. But when he was being Humpty Dumpty he fell off the wall and bumped himself. He began to cry and Mary Mouse had to go on stage and pick him up.

Everyone admired Melia's fairy dance. They laughed at Teddy the Bear when he came on dressed as a clown. He walked right across the stage on his hands and then did a balancing act with a stick, a cup and saucer and a plate. Then he threw balloons to the audience. Peter the

Penguin, Benny the Cat and Pom the
Panda did a funny dance. And at the
end the band played again.
Everyone was sad when the curtain
came down. They clapped and
cheered.

Then Mrs Noah came on the
stage.
"I want to present Mary Mouse,
who thought of this show," she said.
Everyone called for Mary Mouse,

and she went onto the stage and curtsied while everyone clapped.

Then Daddy Doll came out with a big bag of money.

"We have made enough to mend the Ark," he announced.

The next excitement was getting the Ark mended. Everyone helped. Daddy Doll nailed new planks on the deck. Teddy the Bear mended the roof. Pom the Panda and Benny the

Cat painted the sides.

When it was finished, Mrs Noah gave a party. And all the animals helped her to serve guests.

Chapter 8

Pip's Bad Idea

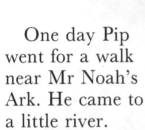

One day Pip went for a walk near Mr Noah's Ark. He came to a little river.

"What fun it would be to dam up this stream just here — and make it go another way!" he thought. "Perhaps if the water went round the Ark, it would float. I'll go and find the others and tell them my idea."

So he went to find Melia, Roundy and the six mice children, Frisky, Scamper, Squeaker, Woffly, Patter and Tiny. They all thought it was a wonderful idea.

They each fetched a little spade and went down to the little river with Pip.

"First we must put earth in the stream, just here," said Pip. So they all began to dig. Soon the dam stretched right across the stream. The water got higher and higher behind the dam. Quickly the children began to dig again. They made a new channel for the water to run down.

"Look, look! The water is leaving the stream and running into our channel!" said Pip.

"Let's stand on the dam we've made and see what happens." said Melia.

She climbed up on to the dam and then *Splash*! She fell head first into the water. Pip pulled her out. She was wet through. Everyone was very frightened.

"We had better take Melia home and dry her," said Pip. So they left the dam and went home.

The water ran down the new channel. Then it overflowed the banks and rushed on towards the Ark! Soon the Ark was surrounded by water.

Mr Noah, Mr Noah! Your Ark is floating on the water. But Mr Noah was fast asleep. Night fell. The moon shone among the clouds. The Ark began to move. Silently it floated away on the water. It went right past the Doll's House. And in the morning, when Mary got up, what a surprise! Mr Noah's Ark had gone! All that was left was the washing line.

"But where have they gone?"
asked Daddy Doll, when Mary told
him.

"They didn't even say goodbye!"
Then Pip began to cry.

"It's all because of us, Daddy," he
wept. "We dammed the stream and

made the water go to the Ark. And then it must have floated away in the night."

"Well, it's no use crying," said Mary Mouse. "We must go and find it."

So off they went, following the new stream, until it joined a big river. Daddy Doll called to a passing steamer:

"Hey, Captain! Have you seen a big wooden Ark?"

The Captain shouted back:

"Yes. It was heading towards a bridge. I hope it won't get stuck underneath."

Well, that was exactly what *had* happened! The Ark had floated on down the river to the bridge. But it was too big to go under it, so there it was, stuck fast!

On board the Ark, poor Mrs Noah was wiping her eyes.

"How did we get here? What-

ever has
happened?"
"We floated
away in the night,"
said Mr Noah. "I don't know how,
though."

Suddenly they heard shouts from
the river bank. It was Daddy Doll
and the others calling to Mr Noah.
All the animals put their heads out
of the windows at once. They knew
Daddy Doll's voice.

"Get your horses, elephants,

tigers, lions, and all your big animals out," called Daddy Doll. "We will harness them to ropes and they can pull the Ark back up the river again."

All the big animals came out of the Ark. Daddy Doll and Mary Mouse put ropes round their necks, and two by two they walked along the riverbank, pulling the Ark along easily.

At last it reached the stream and then came near to the Doll's House. Mr Noah threw down the anchor.

"Well," he said, "I enjoyed that trip so much that I think we will live on the water now, instead of on the land."

So Mrs Noah gave a big party in the Ark to say goodbye to their friends.

Then everyone gave the Ark a push and off it sailed again. And back to the Doll's House went Mary Mouse and Daddy and Mummy Doll and Melia, Pip and Roundy and the six mice children and Whiskers Mouse.

Mary Mouse shut the door. Goodbye everyone, goodbye!

Also in this

series

Book 1   The adventures of Mary Mouse
Book 3   Mary Mouse and the caravan
Book 4   Mary Mouse goes up in a balloon

£2.50
each